Khennaleem

Khennaleem roamed her realm.

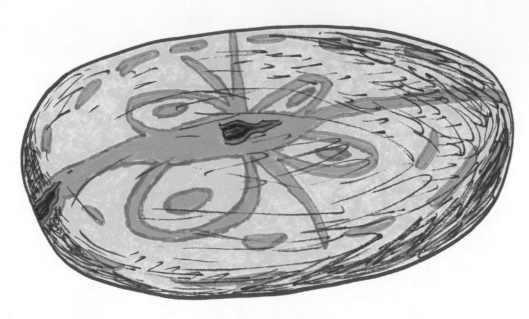

Pristepell

Until she forced higher purpose
upon a pristepell.

Infiniteer Orange

Yet the Cheprotthem, Infiniteer, was infuriated for being created.

Zyphera

So it spewed an infiniteless amount of zypheras
and pushed itself forever into the endless-beneath.

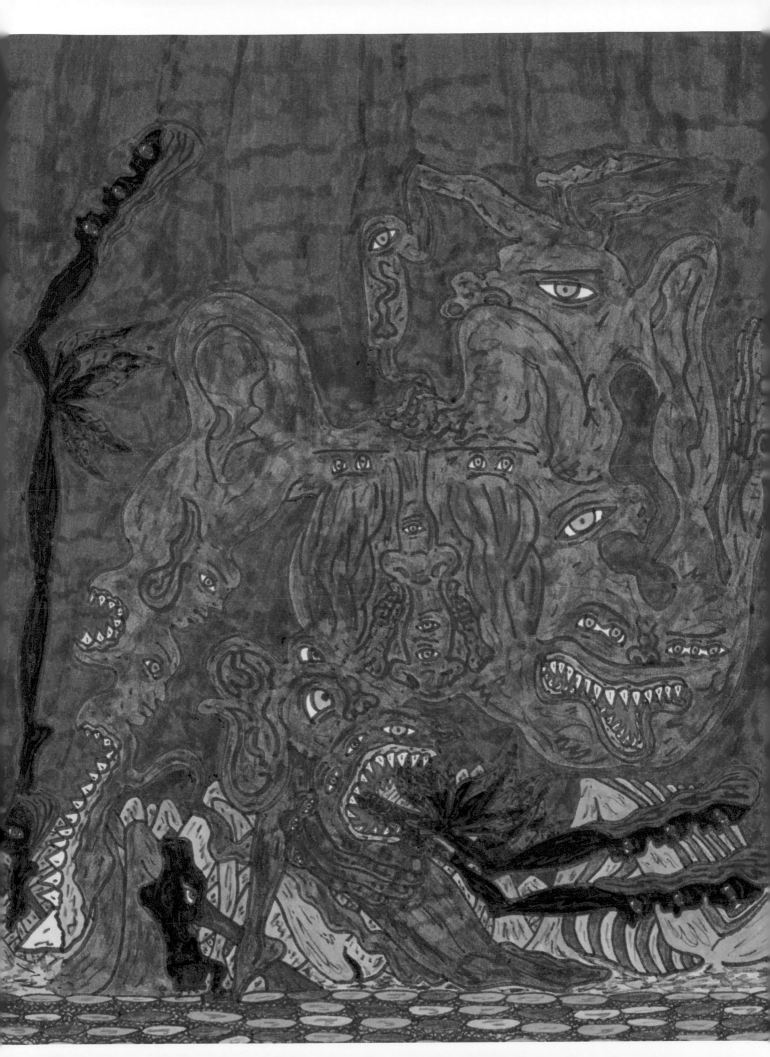

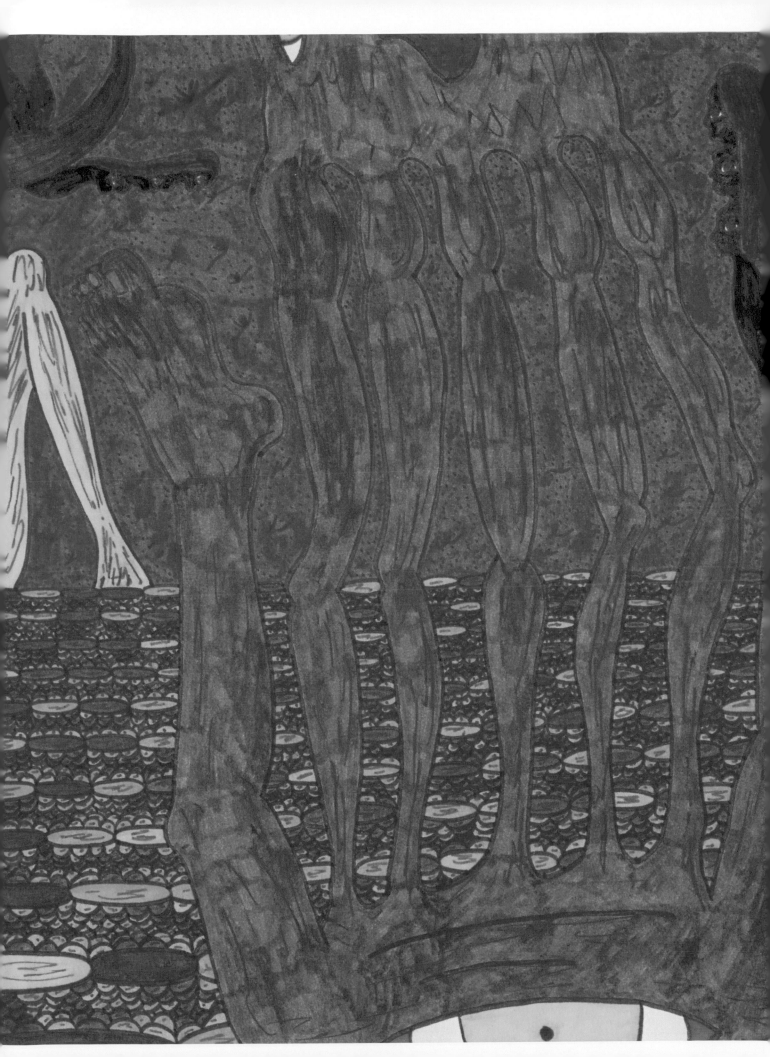

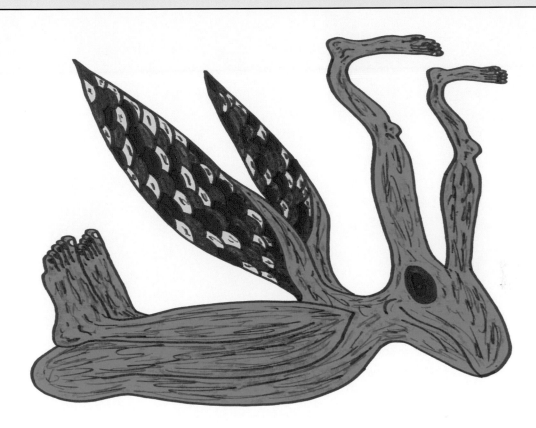

Infiniteer Green

Hurling innumerable pristepell into the sky, the Infiniteer disappeared downward. Khennaleem escaped upon a fleeing zyphera, which touched an ascending pristepell; bringing forth another Infiniteer.

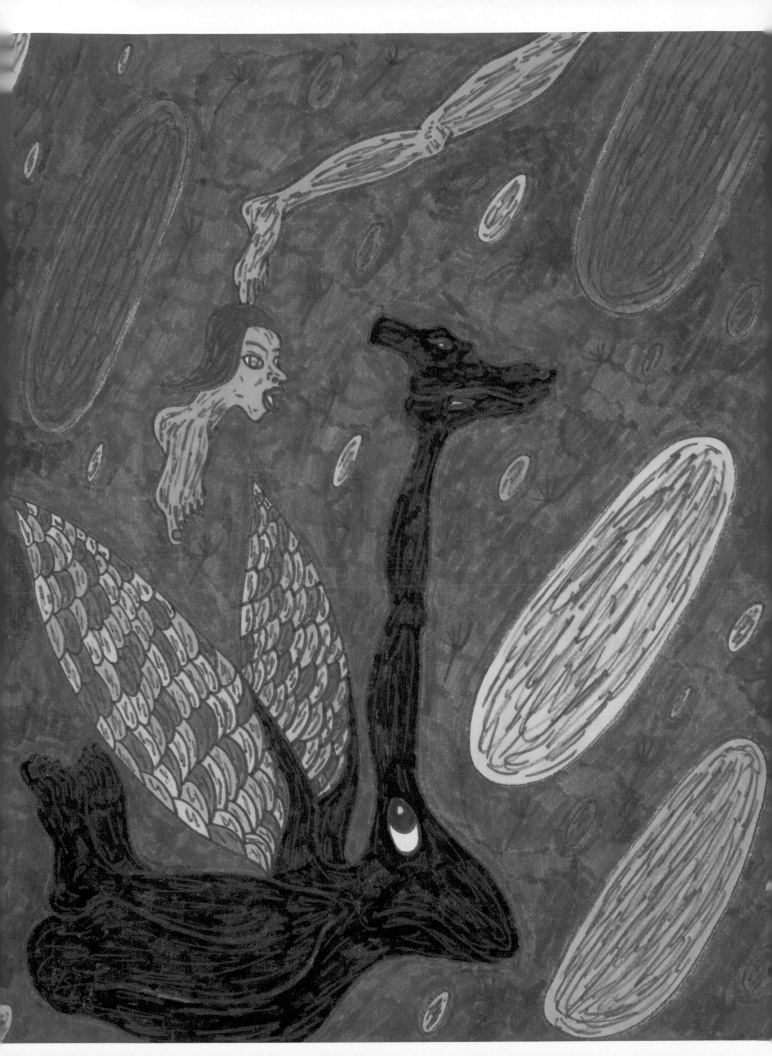

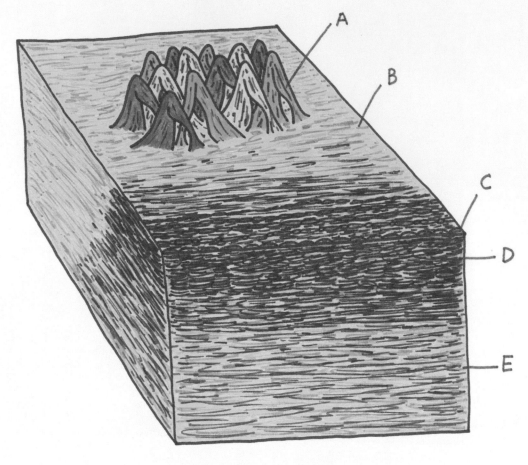

Subsuperveppy

A. Trittle

B. Endless-above (Overinfinite in extension in all directions)

C. Pristepell at endless-above level

D. Pristepell at endless-beneath level

E. Endless-beneath (Overinfinite in extension in all directions, except downward. Downward is only infinite in extension)

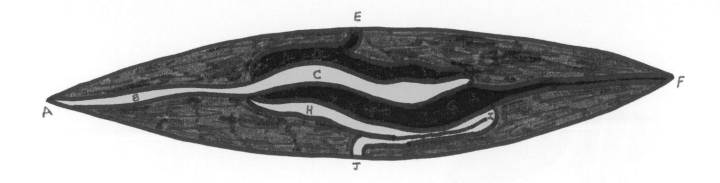

Pristepell Anatomy

A. Vagina Alpha

B. Nexusway Alpha

C. Genesis Alpha

D. Genesis Beta

E. Vagina Beta

F. Vagina Gamma

G. Genesis Gamma

H. Genesis Delta

I. Nexusway Gamma

J. Vagina Delta

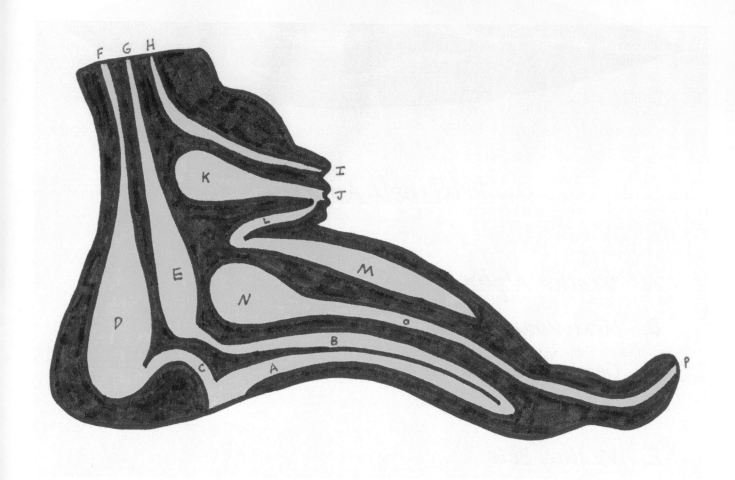

Khennaleem's Anatomy

A. Vagina (Primary)

B. Nexusway Alpha

C. Antevagina

D. Genesis Alpha

E. Genesis Beta

F. Spoutsway Alpha

G. Spoutsway Beta

H. Spoutsway Gamma

I. Nose Vagina (Secondary)

J. Mouth Vagina (Tertiary)

K. Exogenesis Alpha

L. Nexusway Beta

M. Genesis Gamma

N. Exogenesis Beta

O. Grand Nexusway

P. Toe Vagina(s) (Quaternary)

Order this book online at www.trafford.com
or email orders@trafford.com

Most Trafford titles are also available at major online book retailers.

 www.trafford.com

North America & international
toll-free: 844 688 6899 (USA & Canada)
fax: 812 355 4082

Our mission is to efficiently provide the world's finest, most
comprehensive book publishing service, enabling every author to
experience success. To find out how to publish your book, your way,
and have it available worldwide, visit us online at www.trafford.com

ISBN: 978-1-4269-0408-0

Print information available on the last page.

Trafford rev. 03/05/2021

Printed in the United States
by Baker & Taylor Publisher Services